Dzvinka Torokhtushko

THE LITTLE HEDGEHOG

Artist Alexander Kurylo

FAIRY TALES OF THE MAGIC FOREST

Amazon.com

ISBN: 9798354828906

Imprint: Independently published

This is another story of goodness and light. This is a story that teaches us not to be afraid but to overcome even those obstacles that seem insurmountable. Don't be afraid to be small. If you want, you can do everything. For it is not strong who are great and strong physically, but the one who has great strength of spirit and a good heart.

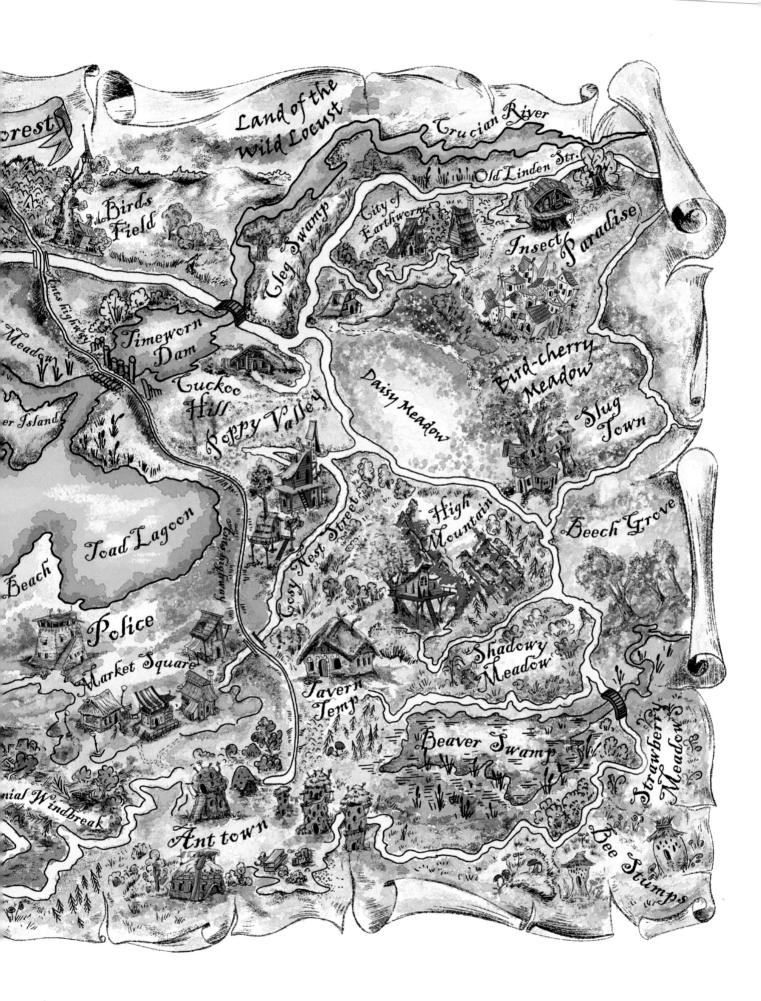

Little Hedgehog woke up because of some strange noise and chumming outside the window. And because his Dad said:

– No, it is not spring yet! Still, have time to take a nap.

Daddy Hedgehog walked around a hut, whistling tender a cheerful tune, squatted, shook his paws, then looked out the window, stretched sweetly and grunted deliciously:

– Hmm! Yeah, it's still early. I'm gonna go to pin a mosquito a little.

And he began to nestle cosily on a cot, pulling a blanket of fluff and autumn leaves up to the very eyes.

– Dad! Don't pin a mosquito! Please, – Little Hedgehog implored. – It buzzes so nice while flying over our river's bank.

– What? What are you saying? – Daddy threw back the edge of the blanket and looked at his son incomprehensively.

– Whom not to pin? – He asked, surprised and sat down so abruptly on the cot that the mattress made of dry needles and inflorescences of willow-herb of old pine sprigs creaked under its weight.

– A mosquito, – Little Hedgehog said quietly. – I like to listen to its singing.

– Oh, my!.. – Mom clapped her paws and laughed. – This is not really, son! It is figuratively. It means to sleep a little or hit the hay.

– Exactly, – Daddy said. – It is not spring yet, and I'll hit the hay while it comes. And you, too.

And he got back to the cot, straightened the blanket, yawned and fell asleep.

– Mommy! – Little Hedgehog went to the window. – And what is spring?

– Spring... Mom smiled dreamily. – Spring... The storks bring it on their wings from the warm lands.

– Isn't it hard for them?

– Oh, surely not! Spring is a warm, gentle wind and a lot of sunlight. Snow melts because of it, then turns into water and runs to our little river. And then snowdrops bloom on the edge of the forest, lungwort, adonis, buds and then leaves appear in the trees, and young grass grows in the meadow.

– Mom, what is snow?

– This is, son, such a white fluffy blanket. The ground sleeps under it all winter long. It is winter now. All nature sleeps under the snow. And we, Hedgehogs, also fall in long winter sleep.

– Until the storks arrive? – Little Hedgehog asked.

– Yes, – Mom replied. – Until the storks arrive and bring spring to us on their wings.

– Mom, is it winter now?

– Winter, – she said and yawned. – Still, time to sleep. A bit more...

Little Hedgehog looked out the window again. However, he didn't see any white blanket there. Only a piece of the trunk of old spruce, under which had their hut was; huge branches right up to the ground, covered with needles; a few cones and last year's fallen needles under them.

– Mom, you say it is winter outside, but there is no snow there. Maybe you and Dad made a mistake? – Little Hedgehog asked.

But Mom had already put her paw under her head and slept sweetly. He wanted to ask something else but changed his mind because he didn't want to wake his Mom up.

Little Hedgehog looked at the window a little more, imagining how, right now, the storks would fly in, carefully remove spring from the wings, and it runs over the edge. And where spring runs, flowers bloom and grass sprout. And dog-rose, apples and wild pears ripen.

Little Hedgehog wanted to eat. Something fresh, tasty, green. However, there were only bundles of dried fruits, mushrooms, and some canned poultry milk in the hut.

Little Hedgehog didn't know how to cook uzvar like Mom, and mushroom roast, which Dad cooked so well. Therefore, he sighed, carefully unwound the stem of the sedge, and removed the wax cap from the can of Mme Cuckoo's poultry milk.

Little Hedgehog took a sip and winced. It wasn't tasted like milk and smelled of rotten hay.

– It's not for nothing that Mme Cuckoo is spoken of pouring water into the milk so it won't turn sour. – Little Hedgehog thought. – She puts the cuckoo flax in the cans.

– Therefore, a blue flower is drawn on the can, – he guessed. And he wanted to share his guesses with someone. But Dad and Mom were sleeping. And he was afraid to go alone to his Granny through the forest. Suddenly, it became noisy and chummy in the street again: the old spruce creaked and swayed. Little Hedgehog was afraid that it would fall and crush their hut. But before he rushed to wake his parents up, the old spruce shook its branches, a cloud of rusty needles appeared below them, and then everything went quiet in the street.

Only the door of the hut trembled, and something clattered behind them. Something very similar to the little hammers that Little Hedgehog saw at carpenter Uncle Woodpecker in autumn.

Little Hedgehog was scared. He wanted to hide under a blanket, pull it over his eyes, close them and lay still. Granny taught him to do so

when it gets scary. She was old and so wise that she knew absolutely everything. At least, Little Hedgehog thought so. Granny said that all children's fears are overcome in this way: hide under the blanket and squeeze the eyes shut. And Grandma's advice always helped.

And Little Hedgehog was already set to flee to his cot. But curiosity – what was ticking outside the door – was stronger than fear.

Little Hedgehog half opened the door. Just for an inch. Precisely, to take a peek and hide at once.

The old spruce's branch leaned to the very threshold. There was something white under it. It trembled and clattered its teeth and then cringed and stared at Little Hedgehog with large shining eyes. Little Hedgehog suddenly remembered his Mom's story about how winter didn't want to retreat before the arrival of spring and how the snow hid at ravines and hollows and between trees' roots so as not to melt.

– So that's what you're like, snow! – Little Hedgehog said.

He stretched his paw through the half-open door and stroked the white, quivering clew.

– Oh! – He exclaimed in surprise. – It's so cold outside, and you're white but warm. So, you will melt soon because spring is just around the corner.

– I'm not snow! – The white clew said. – I'm a bunny. And I won't melt. Just become less noticeable because in spring my fur coat will turn grey.

– By its own? – Little Hedgehog was surprised.

– Yes. Mom will take me to Sunbeam Meadow – it is at the crossroads of Snowdrops and Bilberry Streets. There the sun shines brightly, and the warm spring wind blows. And there, a yellow burr is spreading its leaves faster. The sun's rays are reflected from its brilliant leaves, become sunbeams and jump in the meadow. There, in the reflections of those sunbeams, my fur coat with warm white will turn into a light and grey one.

– May you transform?! – Little Hedgehog asked enthusiastically. – So, as the heroes in fairy tales?

– You can say so, – said Bunny and smiled. – And who are you?

– I am Little Hedgehog; I live here with my Mom and Dad. And my Granny lives at the southern end of the Magic Forest, in Pink Lungwort street.

Bunny touched the needles on the Little Hedgehog's head and twitched back the paw.

– Painfully! – He exclaimed and blew on the paw. – Why do you have such a prickly fur coat?

– I don't know, – Little Hedgehog said. – Probably because I'm a Little Hedgehog. All Hedgehogs have such prickly clothes. And this is not quite a fur coat; it's our weapon against predators.

– Convincingly, – Bunny lightly touched the needles over the Little Hedgehog's forehead. It won't be scary to walk through the forest with you, right? You'll beat all predators with your needles?

– Oh, no! – Little Hedgehog answered. – If a predator wants to eat me, I can only curl up and beat his tongue.

– Cool! – Bunny said. – This is really cool. Cooler than masking with a white fur coat in winter and a grey one in summer.

– You know what? – Bunny said in a minute. – Let's be friends!

– Let's be! – Little Hedgehog agreed enthusiastically.

He went out of the hut and stretched his paw to Bunny.

– Splendidly! – Bunny exclaimed. – In spring, I'll show you a meadow where the most delicious wild carrot grows and a glade with a sweet blackberry.

– And I know where the biggest mushrooms grow in autumn. And I'll show you Oak Ravine. There are as many acorns between the yellow leaves as stars in the sky.

– Oh! Wild boars come there, – Bunny said. – Mom said I must stay out of it.

– But you'll be with me, – Little Hedgehog reassured him. – At once, a boar will appear I curl up like a ball and jump right on it!

– Accurately at round insolent snout! – Bunny exclaimed and stamped his foot.

– Exactly! – Little Hedgehog smiled. He suddenly wanted to be really strong, courageous and... hospitable.

– Probably, you are hungry? Do you want some poultry milk?

– Mme Cuckoo's one? – Bunny winced. – It is tasteless. It's because she dilutes it with water and thickens it with cuckoo flax.

– Yes. Little Hedgehog agreed. – But I have nothing else. Only dried mushrooms and fruits for uzvar. But Mom is still sleeping, and Dad, too. And I don't know how to cook.

– And my Mom had cooked pierogi with cabbage. Bunny sighed and suddenly frowned.

– Mom is probably worried already, – he said in a minute.

– So, go home, – Little Hedgehog advised. – Where do you live?

– At the southern end of the forest, by the stream, – Bunny answered. – Do you know where Vast Water Lily Street is?

– Wow! – Little Hedgehog exclaimed. – It is so far from our Spruce alley! And how did you get here?

– I got lost a little bit, – Bunny said. – I went for a walk and jumped through the puddles to see something interesting. And there are juniper bushes that grow on the edge there. Mom doesn't allow me to go alone there, but I don't on purpose... You see? I've jumped through the puddles and didn't notice how I got to that juniper. And there was someone in the bushes. Trust me – it was. It hid and waited. So disguised that it wasn't visible. But I saw it! Many hungry red eyes were among branches. I was so scared!

– I got you, – Little Hedgehog said. – And who was it?

– I didn't know, – Bunny said, – but I think that since there were many eyes, they probably were boars. Many boars.

Bunny was so agitated that he started to tremble again and clattered his teeth.

– I was very scared. My heart jumped out of my boots. And I rushed with those boots from there. I raced through the forest and didn't look where I ran.

– Oh! – Little Hedgehog exclaimed. – It was really scary. Did the boars run after you?

Bunny took a thought.

– I didn't know. Perhaps they did. All they, all who sat in those bushes. I barely escaped. Came to this spruce and hid.

– You are safe here, – Little Hedgehog reassured him.

You may not be afraid. Let's go to the hut; you'll get warm.

– Thank you, – Bunny said, – but I need to go home. Probably, Mom has already run throughout looking for me. And her pierogi with cabbage... Oh, how I want to eat them!

– So, let's go. Quickly! – Little Hedgehog said.

– I'm afraid to run alone... – Bunny whispered. – Probably, those boars are waiting for me somewhere in the forest. Well, and I don't know the road well.

– Then stay with me. Maybe your Mom will look for you and come here?

– Maybe... Bunny said musingly. – But it won't be soon. And my Mom will worry, and maybe she will even cry.

– Hey, look! – He suddenly started. – Have you ever visited your Granny?

– Yes.

– Would you walk me home? It's not too far. Well, almost next to Pink Lungwort Street.

Little Hedgehog thought about it. He recalled the tangled paths and

trails of the Magic Forest, which gaped with deep holes and potholes from the hooves of deer and moose after winter. He recalled how the forest chairman, Mr Bear, told at the "All-seeing Magpie" radio that while there was a threat of snowing and ice covering, he wouldn't let the workers from the Master Mole company go out for road renovations. For, as the forest dwellers say, it would be monkey toil.

So, instead of roads, there was a complete lack of ways in the Magic Forest before spring. Only boar paths were smooth and pothole-free. Boars laid them with an honest effort and trampled well.

And also, Little Hedgehog recalled how delicious oat flour pies with strawberry fillings his Grandma made. And how long he hadn't seen her. All winter long! Also, she had such a sweet blackberry kissel. And raspberry candies from Mrs Bee's shop.

– Ok, – he said to Bunny, – I would. I'll just leave a note so Mom and Dad don't worry.

Little Hedgehog went back to the hut, took a birch bark roll out of the drawer of the table, tore off a strip from it, took a pigeon feather pointed at the end, dipped it in elder ink and carefully began to draw the letters of the forest alphabet on the bark. Tilting his head to the side, biting his tongue and pressing hard on the pen, as all the animals that had just finished the first class at Mrs Professor Owl's school did.

"Mom and Dad!" – Little Hedgehog wrote. – "I will take Bunny home. He got lost. Do not worry, please. He lives next to our Granny. In Vast Water Lily street. It's very close. Therefore, I'll go to her and spend some time there. Your son, Little Hedgehog."

He re-read what he had written and corrected the letter "g", which was more similar to "y" and resembled a skewed fence near the forest's tavern "Temp", which was next to the Ants highway. There the forest dogbees drank mead and loudly fought all summer long.

While he corrected a letter, an ink drop fell from a feather on birch bark. It spread like an oil spot between words.

Little Hedgehog frowned and wanted to rewrite it all over again. But he remembered that Bunny was waiting for him in the yard. Therefore, he decided to let it be as it was and put the bark in the middle of the table, pinning a corner with a flat stone, as his Dad always did, leaving notes for Mom.

– Let's go! – Little Hedgehog said to Bunny.

– Thank you! – Bunny smiled at him gratefully.

The Little Hedgehog looked around and regretted aloud that it was cloudy outside and there was no sun. After all, it is easier to navigate on it, which side is the northern edge of the forest. But then he looked at the green growth of moss on the trunk of a fir tree, he grinned to himself, and they set off.

They walked along the path trodden by boars, bypassing the fallen trees and gullies. The crowns of tall trees rustled above them. Last year's leaves and dry grass, browned and rusted during the winter, swished under their paws.

Little Hedgehog and Bunny tried to step very carefully. After all, thin, dry branches happened between the leaves, and they could treacherously crack under the weight of steps and attract not quite desirable attention to them.

– You know? – Little Hedgehog said quietly. – You look like a white cloud in this plain, leafless and dark forest.

Bunny laughed loudly. And, as if in response to his laughing, the sky suddenly cleared up. As if some kindly heaven birdie moved heavy clouds with her wings, swept the sky clean, and painted it blue. The sun jumped out of the clouds. Quickly-quickly as a grasshopper on a branch. And flooded, and lighted it with a gentle light.

Little Hedgehog and Bunny stopped to admire the beauty.

– How beautiful! – Bunny exclaimed. – Like in a fairy tale.

– Spring is coming soon... – Little Hedgehog whispered enthusiastically and looked at the sky.

He wanted the storks to fly there right now. The Little Hedgehog dreamed of seeing how they carry spring on their wings to the Magic Forest.

But dark clouds gathered in the sky again and hid the sun. They billowed up like a grey shroud, caught the sun's rays, pushed them deep back and shook the flanks with displeasure, shaking tiny snowflakes to the ground.

Little Hedgehog and Bunny set off. They watched the ground, trees, and bushes covered with white snow.

– Oh! – Little Hedgehog said. – And you are really not seen in the snow.

– That's why I have a winter fur coat, – Bunny said.

The trail sharply turned to the right behind the old raspberry canes. Behind the turn, Old Oak Street began. The forest dwellers called it Tsar's Village and tried to steer clear of it. Because on the right side of Old Oak Street lived: forest mayor Mr Bear, chief police Officer Wolf, charming actress of the "Million Rose" cabaret Lady Otter, forest

prosecutor Mr Elk, public judge Mrs Galeeny, and well-known lawyer Mrs Fox.

And on the left side of the street – several reindeer nouveau-riche, who made a fortune by trading dry moss, bird's fluff and various insulation for the house, settled. And also, there was a whole army of their friends with the poultry milk manufacturer, Mrs Cuckoo, and the sweets seller, Mrs Squirrel, who liked to cheat on the weight of a gullible buyer among them.

Also, in Old Oak Street, an old Rodent lived – a beaver with a somewhat dubious past and unpredictable appetites for the future.

Mr Wolf often detained a beaver for illegally harvesting woods and building dams in public shallows and passed the case to Mrs Galeeny through the prosecutor of Mr Moose. But the lawyer, Mrs Fox, has always found loopholes in the forest laws, messed up Mrs Galeeny's mind, and gave Mr Moose the patter, so the beaver Rodent got away with it.

And also, in Old Oak Street, Mr Lion, nicknamed Tsar, lived out his life. Former times he was a forest mayor, honest and fair. It's said that the beaver Rodent didn't dare to violate forest laws and lived peacefully in a small lake on the edge of the forest.

But it was before. And now Mr Lion has aged and retired. He wanted peace and solitude. Therefore, he settled in the last hut in this street, carried away by embroidering fancy flowers on lily pads and weaving macramé with spider webs.

Sometimes, Mr Lion became tired of his loneliness, so he went out into the street. He waited for a stranger and told him amply about the times that had once been in the forest. It was very impolite to interrupt Mr Lion. And he could talk about the good old times endlessly, spaciously and often repeated. Therefore, the forest dwellers tried to bypass this street to avoid turning into Mr Lion's listeners.

So, in general, respected animals lived in Old Oak Street, rich and honourable. And only Mr Starling, famous brawler, noisemaker and reveller, slightly ruined this idyll. All the time in spring, he returned from warm lands and immediately arranged fights and a mess in the nest; he invited some flighty birds, treated them with the tincture of goji berry, and they laughed loudly and brazenly at the forest inhabitants.

Mr Starling was always dirty, with a chipped beak and a bad temper.

Constantly he pestered everyone, and everything was wrong for him.

But now he was absent, and Old Oak Street was quiet and calm. As soon as the snow began to fall, bullfinches in red aprons appeared in the street and began to sweep the road.

Little Hedgehog and Bunny had admired how the birds deftly were flapping their wings and dispersing the snow and moved on to the edge of the street. And... Oh, my!

It was Mr Lion. He rested gravely on the fence, put his paw as a visor and squinted his lazy eyes, looking for someone walking down the street. His grey-haired but still luxurious mane swayed in the wind; little snowflakes entangled between wool, and Mr Lion seemed even older and more respectable.

– Hmm, do you know? – Mr Lion exclaimed happily. – Everything was different when I, a tiny lion cub, moved from a faraway savannah to the Magic Forest. It wasn't like this before! Whoever heard of it, and where is Mr Bear watching?! As long the world is the world, and the forest is the forest, spring comes in time. And now looks like the world

 **23**

turned upside down! It is already Spring on the calendar, and the forest is covered with snow! When I was a forest mayor, it wasn't like this! Well, I will tell you...

At that moment, the wind started to blow harder, the snow went tight, and the wind turned it into a white cloud. And, having hidden in it, Little Hedgehog and Bunny rushed past Mr Lion.

– Ahoy! – Mr Lion shouted after them. – Where are you?

But Little Hedgehog and Bunny were already far away.

– It seems I had a vision, – Mr Lion thought aloud and again raised his paw to his eyes, peering into the road.

– Phew! Get lucky! – Little Hedgehog sighed relief.

– Exactly! – Bunny agreed. – They say that Mr Lion may talk to anybody's end.

They continued travelling across Duckweed Lagoon, by the old stumps in which someone still lived, through Chamomile Meadow and Pine Glade.

The lagoon was small, narrow, but very deep. It was impossible to ford it, and there was nothing on the lakeside to cross to that side.

Also, it would be unwise to bypass the lake around. The lake was big and even huge for Little Hedgehog and Rabbit.

And, besides, they were almost to the southern edge of the Magic Forest.

– We'll have to come back, – Bunny sighed, – and somehow get through the "Master Mole" team and their barricades.

– I'm completely frozen, – Little Hedgehog said, – but what can we do? Let's go. We'll get home – get warm.

– Wait, where do you think you're going? – An unpleasant squeaky voice from the reed thickets on the lake sounded. – Huh, peanuts?

– Grunt-grunt-grandiose! – Someone responded nearby. – Oh, how squeal-squeal-queenly lunch we'll have, bro! Oink-oink-royal lunch!

From the reed marshland, two burly boars came out. They had thick and long stubble on their heads, with predatory hungry eyes and sharp fangs.

– You are right! – The second one agreed. – But, at least, it will be stuck in a tooth.

– Oh! – Bunny shivered. – How scary they are! They will eat us up!

Little Hedgehog also thought so and wanted to run. But then he remembered that he had recently promised Bunny he could protect him from wild boars. After all, Bunny is utterly helpless in front of them in his white fur coat while he has needles. And he can curl up and...

– Run! – Little Hedgehog shouted. – Run as fast as you can!

– Squeak-squeak-dreaming! – the Boar squeaked, hit the ground with his hoof, bent his head and moved straight at Little Hedgehog.

When Boar and Little Hedgehog were over a short distance, Little Hedgehog looked into Boar's hungry red eyes, pushed his hind paws and jumped, curling up into a spiky tangle on the fly. And he got right into the pink boar snout.

The Boar grunted, bulged his eyes even more, filled with tears immediately, and stomped his hooves on the ground.

– You broke my no-oink-oink-nose! – He squealed at the whole forest.

– I'll rip you to shreds! – The second Boar yelled and rushed to Little Hedgehog.

Little Hedgehog jumped again, curled up in the air and dug into the Boar's snout with needles. He fell, sunken his wounded snout in the snow.

– I will deal with you! – The Boar yelled.

Little Hedgehog grouped again. And he glanced at the spot where Bunny stood.

But Bunny was standing still there and trembling with fear.

– Run! – Little Hedgehog exclaimed.

But Bunny stood still, motionless.

– Come on, run! Do you hear me? Run as fast as you can! – Little Hedgehog shouted. – I'll hold them up!

– No need, little chap! – Somebody's calm but assertive voice sounded next to them. – It's okay, Little Hedgehog! I'll detain them.

The chief policeman of the Magic Forest, Mr Wolf, proudly stepped out from the willow arrays growing on the lake shore. The Wolverine, forest guards, followed him in his footsteps.

– And for a long time! – Mr Wolf barked.

– What? Why? We just had grunt-grunt-grand fun. – The Boars exclaimed in one voice.

– Really?! – Mr Wolf howled loudly. – Had fun?

– Exactly, – the Boars grunted.

– And when you stole a barrel of heady barley from a tavern "Temp" located near the Ant Highway, you crawled to dig the shore illegally in

reed marshes to get crayfish for that barley – did you have fun, too?

– We want to see a lawyer! – The Boars shouted.

– I'm here! – Mrs Fox said. – I'm at your service. Of course, if you may pay for it.

– Oh, yes! – The Boars gladly nodded their heads. – We know where the quails are hiding.

– Perfect! – Mrs Fox happily rubbed her paws and put a sharp ear with a shiny birch earring just to the Boar's snout.

The Boar quickly whispered a word to her, and Mrs Fox licked her lips.

– So, Mr Chief Police, – Mrs Fox solemnly said, – I demand a softer and more, so to say, animality handling with my clients. And I have enough arguments and evidence that testify to their innocence and law-abidingness.

– All your evidence to the dog's tail! – Mr Wolf roared. – I meant to wolverines, not dogs. All you say, it's just as true as the fleas may bark!

– Mr Wolf, as an attorney for these honourable beasts, I declare that I won't admit any abuse! You'll have to answer by the laws of the Magic Forest for illegal detention.

– Mme lawyer, – Mr Wolf looked at her fixedly, – they were caught red-handed.

– It's not true! – Mrs Fox smiled. – Boars have hooves, not hands.

– Mrs Fox! – Mr Wolf roared. – You'll be responsible for giving false testimony in our Magic Forest's Main Court. All your arguments to the wolverines!

– We-e-ell! – Mrs Fox said protractedly. – You

know better, Mr Wolf. You are Law and Order here. To wolverines? So, let it be!

She winked coquettishly, waggled her long, luxurious tail and quickly disappeared into the willows.

– Why "to wolverines"? – The Boars started to protest. – You promised! And quails? We told you where they hid! It's a failure!

– It's a victory! – Mr Wolf bellowed. – Wolverines, delay them immediately! Today they'll stay in a forest pit, and tomorrow Mrs Galeeny, the judge, will verdict, and they go to dig ditches from the pit in Crested Thistles Street till the river. Since it's half of the street is already flooded because of that pit. Wolverines surrounded the boars and took them deep into the forest. The boars gloomily followed them.

– You're great, Little Hedgehog! – Mr Wolf said. – A true hero and a true friend.

– Oh, yes, Mr Wolf! – Bunny said with a still trembling voice. – I am so glad I met Little Hedgehog, and he became my friend. He is so brave and strong!

– Well, heh! – Mr Wolf said. – He has as much power as a sparrow under his knee. But he has enough courage and dexterity. Join me when you grow up; you will be a forest guard. Or whom do you want to be?

– Little Hedgehog, – Little Hedgehog said and blushed when he felt he had said something wrong, – but the guard, too, – he corrected himself.

– Well, let it be! – Mr Wolf laughed. – And now, where do you go?

– I am escorting Bunny home, – Little Hedgehog said. – And then I'll go to my Granny.

– Sit on my back; I will take you there. – Mr Wolf suggested putting his paws down so it would be easier for Little Hedgehog and Bunny to climb onto his back.

– Amazing! – Little Hedgehog said on the way. – We're going on the wolf's neck. Has it ever been like this?

– We're both like in a fairy tale. – Bunny said.

– Oh! – Mr Wolf exclaimed. – Our former mayor, Mr Lion, nicknamed Tsar, may tell you, for sure, that this has never happened before.

– Indeed, – Little Hedgehog agreed.

Wolf drove them quickly to the hut in Vast Water Lily Street. From the burrow ran out excited Bunny's Mother, grabbed her baby and hugged him tightly.

– Where have you been, my Bunny? I have worried so much!

– Sorry, Mom. – Bunny whispered. – I will tell you everything later.

But Bunny had to tell immediately. Since the forest radio's presenter "All-seeing Magpie" had heard such news, she immediately flew to do a report. Bunny stumbled a bit, hesitated, but honestly told about their incident with Little Hedgehog. And soon, all the inhabitants knew that

Little Hedgehog was a true hero and friend. Everyone admired Little Hedgehog and made an example of him to their children.

And only two boars grunted angrily in a deep forest pit:

– Oink-oink! How they had promoted those cubs!

Bunny's Mom fed him and Little Hedgehog with still warm pierogi with cabbage. And then she and Bunny took Little Hedgehog to his Granny to Pink Lungwort Street.

Granny Hedgehog just finished knitting a new beret with mohair threads. And before, as if foreknow that the guests would come, she had baked many oatmeal pies. With strawberry filling. Grandma was pleased to see Little Hedgehog. And when Bunny's Mother told her about the cubs' adventures, she was even gladder and very proud of Little Hedgehog.

– That's who you are! – Grandmother said proudly. – The real Little Hedgehog!

And she regaled everyone with the yummiest uzvar ever with pies; gave the Bunny's Mom several sweets recipes; showed new patterns with web threads, and told her one big-big secret. The fact is that cabbages should be planted only with a full moon. Then its heads will be big and round. For if you plant it when the moon is sickle, then its heads will crack.

– You are welcome in spring. – Bunny said for goodbye. – You are a true friend and a real defender. You're cool!

– Whoa! – Little Hedgehog blushed.

– You are not just cool – you are the coolest! And I'll definitely show you where the sweetest wild carrots grow in the forest.

– I will come. – Little Hedgehog promised. – I will come when the real spring comes.

– Thank you. – Bunny smiled happily.

– A little bit more – and there will be a real spring. – Granny said.

But Little Hedgehog didn't hear her already. He jumped on the cot and quickly fell asleep. Grandma covered him with a warm blanket of alder leaves and swan fluff.

She whispered quietly:

– Sleep, my dear! Good night, sleep tight!

And at this time, Little Hedgehog was already dreaming of storks over the forest. They carried spring on their wings. Warm, ringing and colourful. Spring's drops fell from the stork's wings to the ground. And wherever they fell, green grass pushed out, and flowers bloomed.

And on Sunbeam Meadow, warm rays of the spring sun have reflected off dew drops on the cowslip leaves and jumped out with bright highlights in the air.

And across that glade, Little Hedgehog's friend Bunny jumped. In a light grey fur coat. The sunrays sparkled on a new fur.

– How nice! – Little Hedgehog whispered in a dream.

– Very nice! – Granny smiled at him. And started to sew down motley magpie feather to her new beret from the threads of a mohair web. That feather that reporter of "All-seeing Magpie" radio had lost, and Bunny's Mom picked up. And then went and forgot it.

– It's not good to waste goods. – Little Hedgehog's Granny thought loudly.

The old lady pulled out the needle upper her eye, which had bothered her because it was longer than the others. She put a web thread into the needle and sewed a feather on the beret's brim. You know, on the side, from left, so that everyone could see how beautiful she was and... how did Bunny say? The coolest? That's right! Beautiful and the coolest Granny of Little Hedgehog-the-hero!

THE END!

Dzvinka Torokhtushko

THE LITTLE HEDGEHOG

Artist Alexander Kurylo

ISBN: 9798354828906

Imprint: Independently published

Made in the USA
Monee, IL
29 October 2022

16633595R00024